Mayhem Carnival

Scarlett Swan

Copyright © 2023 by Scarlett Swan

All rights reserved.

No portion of this book may be reproduced in any form without written permission from the publisher or author, except as permitted by U.S. copyright law.

ISBN: 9798865654872

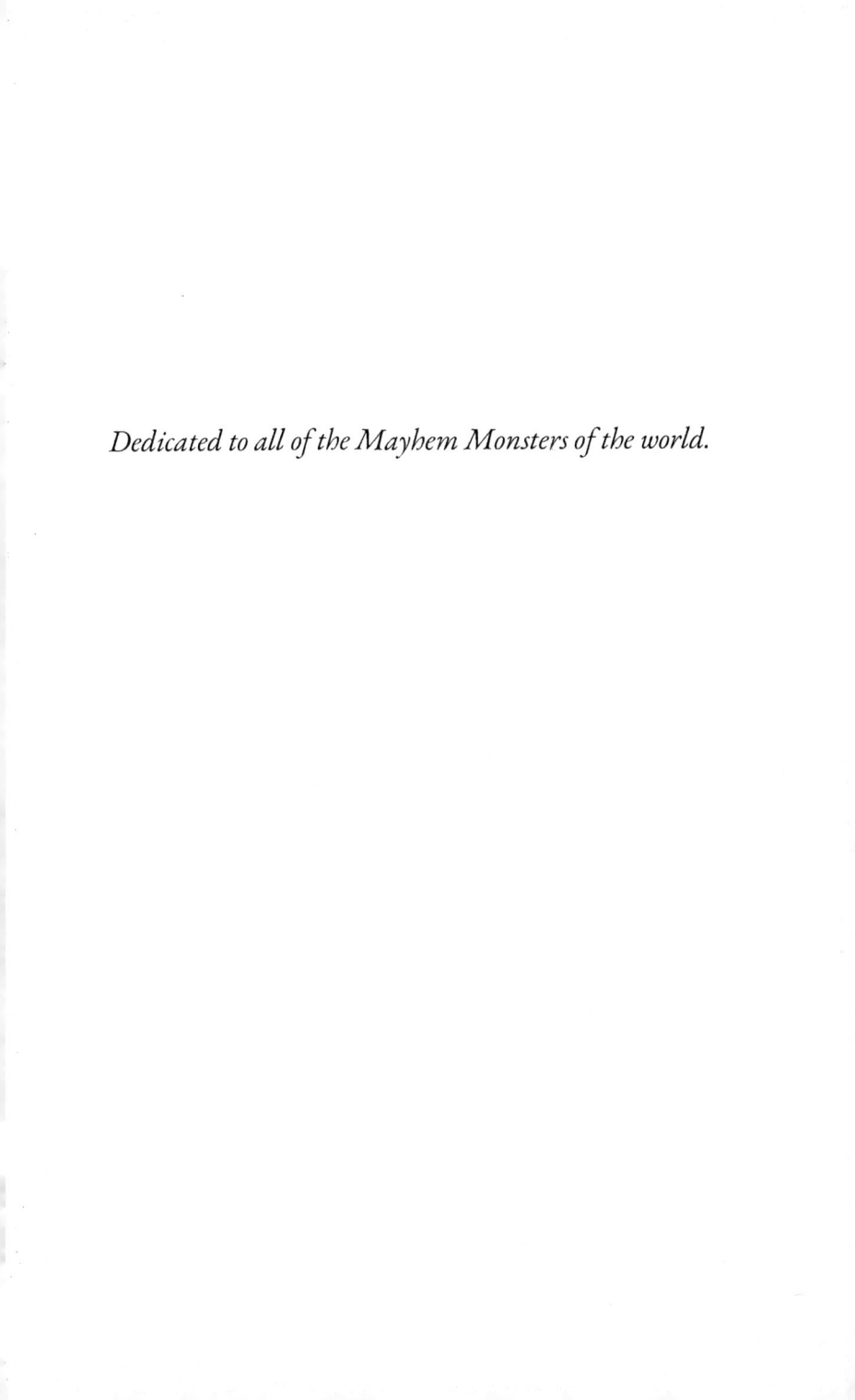

Dedicated to all of the Mayhem Monsters of the world.

Come one, come all.

MAYHEM
CARNIVAL

PLAYLIST

1. SLAYER - BRYCE SAVAGE
2. HALLOWEEN - THE MISFITS
3. BLINDING LIGHTS - THE WEEKEND
4. LOSE CONTROL - TEDDY SIMS
5. MONSTER - LADY GAGA
6. SOMEBODY'S WATCHING ME - ROCKWELL
7. CREEP - RADIOHEAD
8. CALL ME - BLONDIE
9. HALLOWEENIE - ASHNIKKO
10. KILL BILL - SZA
11. BAD GUY - BILLIE EILISH
12. ARSONIST'S LULLABYE - HOZIER

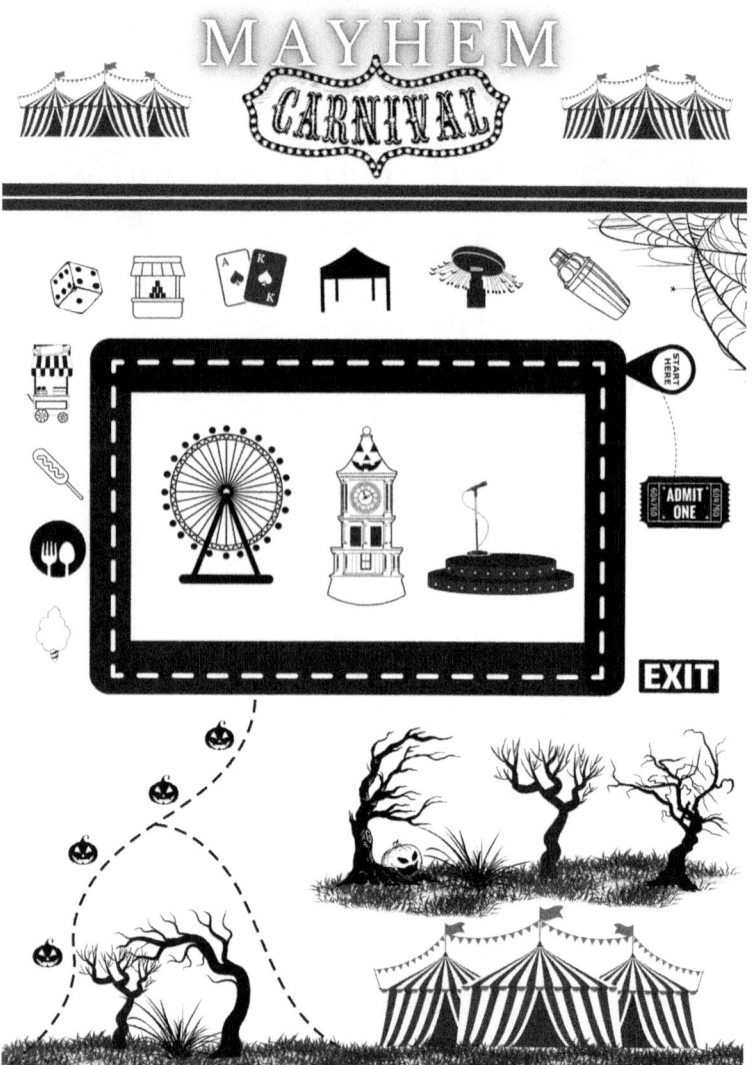

One

The carnival appears once a year on Halloween.
 The location is always different, but the party is the same.
The promise of a night of pure euphoria.
Mayhem is by invitation only.
This year, I was invited.
Tonight, is going to be fucking insane.
Mandy – my best friend and roommate - is getting ready, sliding a juicy apple red over her plumped lips. "I heard there would be no point in that." I tease her.
She tilts her head, grinning at me. "I think men quite like it when you've got lipstick smeared all over your face because you've sucked them off."
I don't argue with that, instead I decide between wearing

a mini skirt or dress. I opt for the skirt, it's black and flowy but short enough that when I walk people can see the goods.

For my shirt, I pick a baby blue crop top. No bra, but I do pluck a pair of black, lacy panties from my drawer. I'm sure they'll be off of me in no time, but it's fun to know someone will take them.

I stare at my reflection while Mandy gawks at me. "Kels, you look fucking hooootttt!"

Her admiration makes me grin. I run my matte black stiletto nails through my pin-straight blonde hair, admiring the way the skirt fits my curvy frame. Other girls have always been obsessed with their weight, but not me. I sit at five foot three and weigh one hundred ninety pounds, I've found that men love that.

But I love me some thinner girls too, Mandy for instance is a bombshell. Nearing six foot tall, with the longest legs you've ever seen and striking red hair that matches her fiery personality.

She needs that spice with her being a defense lawyer and all.

I work for a Fortune 500 company, as the assistant to a very hot, very wealthy CEO.

We both have extremely intense and stressful work environments, so when we woke up a month ago to invitations slid underneath our door to Mayhem we freaked out.

I'm not sure how they select their candidates but two

years ago we submitted an application to attend. They must have vetted us, watched us, all this time, and now is finally our chance.

Even after getting our wax-sealed envelopes, we had some work to do. There are rules as to who can attend.

All guests must pass an STI test.
All guests must be over the age of 21.
Participants are aware that they will be touched, fondled, fucked.
- with their consent, of course. -
No phones.

The workers are titled Mayhem Monsters, you will notice them not only for their striking good looks, but each Monster wears a glowing bracelet made specifically for this event.

The monsters are there for your pleasure, any and all explicit activities between guests is strictly prohibited - with the exception of your party.
There are enough monsters to go around.

· · ·

Then there was the NDA, a ton of legal jargon that Mandy handled for me because it sounded like a language that didn't exist.

Basically, no photos or videos, no phones, or any type of recording equipment. Nothing that could prove what's going on behind the exclusive gates of Mayhem. From what I've heard, they pay a *very* hefty amount to the city officials in the place they decide to choose. The allure of such a mystery excites me to my core.

"Ready?" Mandy asks, spraying a bit of perfume in the air.

I slip on my heels, knowing I'll be regretting the choice later, but they look so good, how could I not?

I imagine all the possibilities tonight could bring, but nothing can truly prepare you for Mayhem.

Two

"So, what is it we have to do?" I ask Mandy, fiddling with my nails. With no phone, I'm a little out of my element. Our whole lives revolve around the stupid little thing. Mandy's holding hers though, always the planner. I'm more of a go-with-the-flow type.

We needed it to track our Uber but at the gate they'll be searching us and taking it.

"So," Mandy tosses her long hair across her shoulder, tapping a heel on the sidewalk. "Our ride will be here in five minutes. Then, they'll take us to these coordinates." She shows me the image on her phone.

I laugh, "Is this a military operation?"

"Seriously, these directions are insane. When the Uber drops us off, we'll be put into another car that will take us to the carnival."

"Will we be blindfolded?" I joke.

"Yes." She deadpans.

The realization that we're going to have no phones at a place we were invited to by complete, horny strangers is unnerving.

Mandy notices my anxiety. "This is why I didn't say anything." She rubs my shoulder, letting out a small sigh. "We're okay. This is the safest, most fun night you will ever experience. They've done their research on us, and I've dug into a few client files to read up on them." She whispers, although no one is around.

A gasp escapes me, "Mandy!" I whisper back in a scandalous tone.

"I didn't find much." She continues, "But we had a client whose wife went three years ago and he was pissed. Too rich for his own good, so he funneled everything into finding who runs it."

"Did he?"

She bellows out a laugh, "No. All we learned was that this carnival has been in operation dating back to the seventies. The cops and FBI tried to catch them long ago, so they moved out of the country. Then the worries died down and the carnival came back to the States. It's a safe, long-standing organization, and we're going to let our guard down and have fun."

"Plus, they pay off everyone in the counties they run," I

add, sucking in a deep breath, knowing at least we shouldn't have to deal with the threat of jail time. "Just no separating, okay?"

"Of course! And once we're done we'll be back here and snuggling into those semi-comfy beds." She laughs, gesturing to our Airbnb.

Typically, we're city girls. Two thirty-somethings sharing an apartment in New York, but of course where it's a traveling sex carnival, we had to journey to it.

Which is fine with us, we needed the break. We're staying at a cute little place in the countryside of South Carolina. All the homes are decorated with smiling jack-o-lanterns, cotton webs, and orange lights.

It's Halloween eve, and typically I would be freezing in the city but here it's nice and warm, with a breeze that makes my skin tingle.

The thoughts of tonight circle in my mind. There isn't much I know but what I do have knowledge of from the invitation is that the Mayhem Monsters are there for our pleasure. I've never experienced anything like this.

Before I can think about turning back, the Uber pulls up and I step in, abandoning any fears I may have.

Tonight is about letting loose.

A night of pure, delightful mayhem.

Three

If our handsome driver knew what we were about to experience, he would surely be blushing. He's cute, in his mid-thirties, and completely oblivious that he's driving us to a location to essentially be blindfolded and kidnapped, taken to an unknown location to fuck our brains out.

This is already so much fun!

"A little old school to be giving out coordinates." He jokes as Mandy holds the screen to him, illuminating his sharp features.

Mandy laughs, "It's cool, right?"

"It is old school." I agree with him.

"Where are you two ladies heading tonight?" he asks, pulling down the street.

We both pass a glance at each other, "We're going

Geocaching." Mandy sticks to the storyline that was prompted in the instructions.

He tilts his head in inquiry, "It's an app where you get sent random coordinates, and they lead you to a treasure of some sort at a cool location." I elaborate and he nods, turning up the volume of his radio.

The rest of the ride is spent with Mandy and I singing along to nineties pop music that our driver has so graciously put on. As we pull off onto a dusty road, we both quiet down.

Up ahead I see people wearing illuminated masks that remind me of The Purge. The driver turns the radio off. "They joining you?" He asks wearily, leaning his head back a bit.

A nervous laugh escapes me. "Umm..." I wasn't prepared to be answering questions I don't know the answer to. For the carnival to be so secretive it's funny they let Uber drivers see them creepily standing in the woods.

The closer we get the more my heart flutters. There are five of them, standing by a few glossy black Escalades.

Their heads are tilted menacingly, but if anything, it makes me want to jump their bones more. Black pants, no shirt, and *those masks*. Father forgive me for I'm about to sin.

I want to be fucked by all five of them while they wear those damn masks. The thought of it has me rubbing my legs together until I remember we're in an Uber and the man is staring at me waiting for an answer.

"I'm fucking with you. I work with Mayhem." He finally says. "I'll be back to get you two when the gates close." He sends us a wink and we step out. "Have fun you two."

Mandy grabs my hand, "Holy fucking shit, Kels."

"I know dude." I breathe out, *I know.*

"Hello, ladies." The second man is speaking, his mask a fiery neon red, dark skin glistening under the moonlight.

"How is all Hallows Eve working out for you?" That was the first one, sporting a green mask that frowns.

"Are you ready for Mayhem?" The third asks. He stands out among the illuminated masks of his friends. I let out a sharp intake of breath as his long legs bring him directly in front of me with two quick strides. Six feet tall, he cranes his neck to look down at me. His mask has two X's for eyes and a stitched smile that creeps to both ends. It casts my face in a bright, neon blue.

I breathe in his earthy scent as his tattooed finger crooks underneath my chin, forcing me to look up at him. "I'm going to need you to turn around." He growls.

The way he said it reminds me of law enforcement and I wonder for a moment what these men do for their day jobs. He doesn't wait for me to answer and when he turns me around and clasps both of my wrists in one hand, I know exactly what he does.

"Calm down officer." I tease.

He brings his face closer to mine, the plastic of his mask cold against my cheek. Don't make me handcuff you and fuck you right here in front of everyone." He warns. There's an edge to his voice that makes me heat to my core. I wish he would handcuff me, but he doesn't. He's just holding my wrists together, using one of his large hands.

I take a glance at Mandy, who's busy flirting with two of the men.

My guy places a silk blindfold gently over my face. "Is that too tight?" He asks in a kind voice.

"No, it's perfect." I tell him in a sultry tone. He gently guides me to what I assume is the side of the Escalade.

"Hands up." He purrs.

Oh, I'm getting searched right here. I place my hands on the cool glass and relish in the feel of his hands thoroughly touching every single inch of my body with the swift movements of a man who knows exactly what he's doing. Aside from the goods, which makes me a little sad. "You can check everywhere." I assure him.

"Oh, I'm going too. Don't you worry, princess." He laughs, it's low and sexy.

Both of his large, inked hands cup my breasts. Without the sense of sight, the sensation of his hold on me intensifies, making me grow wetter. He purrs as he reaches down, rubbing his hand gently over my pussy. Teasing me. "She's been checked." He tells the others.

He ushers me into the back seat of the car. "Where's Mandy?" I ask.

"She's getting in right now." He buckles me in, although I have the mobility of my hands and could do it myself. His body leaning over mine sets my nerve endings on fire.

I hear the other door open. Mandy is flirting still. "Fuck me later?" She asks one of them. I'm so glad that we are comfortable enough around each other to do something like this together.

We met at a club about seven years ago, and ever since we've been inseparable. It was a sex club, which explains a lot about us, but I wouldn't change a thing.

The doors close with a loud thud, leaving us in the quiet car.

I reach my hand over to hers. "I'm so excited."

"I'm freaking the fuck out." She breathes in and out. "We could literally just stay here with them and I would be happy."

I think of the sexy guy in the blue mask, with his deep voice and the way he towered over me. I can still feel his strong, capable hands on my skin. "I wish he would have just taken me right there as he searched me."

"If that's what you want, I'll be sure to find you later

Kelsey." His familiar tone purrs. Hearing him say my name sends me into another dimension. A blush rises to my cheeks. He's the driver and I am mortified but also excited that he may be telling the truth and we could have a little fun later.

Maybe it's the anticipation of waiting impatiently for months to experience this night ever since we received our invitations, but I'm drawn to this man instantly.

MUSIC BLARES in the car as we dip and turn down curvy roads, unable to see what's ahead of us. We are not in control at all, and I love it.

Ten minutes later, we come to a stop.

The door opens. I'm being unbuckled and ushered out of the car. The first thing that hits me is the smell of salty air, mixed with a tingly cedar and a warm breeze that blows my hair.

The blindfold is untied, it's smooth fabric slipping down my face. The man in the blue mask is standing before me, head tilted. I look up at him, smiling, then I look past him. My line of vision tells me two things.

1. We're at a harbor.
2. The gate is right behind him.

It's a large, ornate, wrought iron gate. Covered in lights, webs, and skulls. I can see the water in the distance, some lighting, but not much else. The mystery of it all is so enchanting to me.

"Time?" I ask Mandy.

She shrugs, "They've got my phone." She gestures to the delectable man who has now taken my hand in his.

"It's eleven on the dot." He tells me, ushering us both to the gate.

The party begins at midnight, but the invited guests can come and enjoy the carnival all day long. We didn't want to tire ourselves out, but we also didn't want to miss the transition, so we decided to come just a little bit early. "I'm Creed, by the way."

Hot guy name. *Check.* "My name's Kelsey, but everyone calls me Kels," I laugh, "but you already knew that."

His inked hand leaves mine to grip the heavy gate. The hum and creak of the doors opening welcomes us. Creed's muscles bulge and strain against the pull, his hand swoops in front of him and as I step inside, he grips my arm, pulling me tight against his chest.

He lifts his mask, only slightly enough to show me his chiseled jawline and pearly white grin. "I meant what I said. I'll find you later if you'd like." He plants a kiss on my cheek before pulling his mask back down.

Mandy grips my arm and pulls me away. "I'd like that!" I shout as we rush away on the concrete path, lined with tall trees. The branches crane down and out towards us, covered in string lights that ignite the beautiful pathway in rich, amber light. Just ahead is the ticket counter.

The thought of Creed coming for me later feeds my insatiable fire. To see his eyes under the mask, I wonder what color they are. To run my hands through his hair as his strong arms lift me up against a wall.

But who am I kidding, he probably flirts with all of the girls. Five hundred dollars a ticket probably pays a good salary for the workers.

A GRAND ARCH that's dripping in lights sits right beyond the ticket counter. We're bouncing on our heels as we step up. "May I have your invitations?" A beautiful woman in black lingerie asks.

Her stiletto nails take them and she examines every inch carefully. "Kelsey and Mandy." She reaches into a box and pulls out two pink silk bands and ties them on our wrists, then hands us a map. "remember ladies, midnight is when we all come out to play." She bites her lip, her attention pointed directly at Mandy.

"Can't wait!" Mandy sings.

Stars twinkle overhead as we walk underneath the enormous Mayhem Carnival sign, smothered in glittering lights.

A kaleidoscope of colors, scents, and sounds surrounds us.

My heart flutters with anticipation, and I can't help but feel a rush of excitement as I clutch Mandy's hand. The aroma of sweet cotton candy and buttery popcorn wafts through the air, making my stomach groan.

"Are you ready for this?" I ask, a wide grin on my face.

Mandy nods, her eyes shining with a mix of lust and wonder. "So fucking ready but I wish we knew the time." She says impatiently.

No phone, no watch... I peer around the vast space. Finding a clocktower that's covered in spiderwebs and Halloween décor. "Eleven twenty." I point to it. Time seems to be moving incredibly slow, but I have a feeling that when the clock strikes midnight the night will speed past in a blur. I want to soak in every second of this forbidden place.

I look down at my silk band, noting a QR code on the end.

The best part about the carnival is that our ticket price is all-inclusive. We can eat, drink, ride whatever ride and whoever we want. It's an adult playground. "Liquor?" She asks. I eagerly agree, and we make our way over to the line, chatting and laughing as we go.

The booth is made to look like a giant ice cube. Blue and white lights radiate from underneath the bottles of high-end liquor on the shelves behind the workers. "What do you want?" Mandy asks, surveying the menu in front of us. There are all kinds of delicious-looking drinks. The names are a glimpse of what tonight is going to be like.

I step up to the sexy, muscular bartender who's dressed in a slim portion of firemen gear, just the suspenders and pants. Noting the ice block in the center that's in the shape of an ace of spades. "Doggy Style please." I laugh.

The man expertly tips the bottle of vodka at the top left of the ice block. The liquid maneuvers around the spade and down to the middle. The rest of the descent slithers in a sweeping motion, sliding through like a river until it lands in my glass.

He adds in the freshly squeezed fruit juices, topping it with a garnish. Mandy gets a Sex On The Beach which is her usual beverage of choice on any given Friday night.

I tip my drink back, tasting the fruity hints of grapefruit and blackberry as they dance on my tongue. "Oh my god." I moan, "This is dangerous. Essentially an open bar, I'm going to have to be careful tonight."

"I know!" She agrees, "This all feels like some kind of fever dream."

I pull the map from my pocket, wanting to not only pass the time but get familiar with the area. I'm never a planner, but if any night I am going to be, it's tonight.

Imagine a rectangle, the entrance where we are is on the short side. To the right is the harbor on the long stretch of road. A large 'Enter if you dare' sign sits at its opening. That street houses rides, drinks, and other surprises.

The other short end is where all of the food and games await. I'm so excited to see what those are!

Then the last street, the other long one is where the Haunted Houses and Carnival are at.

The middle is where the clock tower and enormous Ferris Wheel are.

'Fun awaits at every corner.' The map reads at the bottom.

"Ten more minutes!" We could venture in further, but I want to be right here when everything starts.

We head to a section of small tables with flickering candles to the right of the booth.

You can feel the tension in the air as the clock's minute hand inches closer and closer to midnight. I nudge Mandy's arm when I notice people emerging from the darkness of the woods, illuminated by slivers of moonlight that fight to break through the winding trees.

They're coming towards the gates, surrounding us. Donning various masks and costumes, glistening abs, and an aura of danger with them. Women in lingerie slink through the trees and around the men, looking like fierce lionesses. Their faces covered with masquerade masks.

The Mayhem Monsters are making their way to us slowly, purposefully. I fidget with the drink in my hand, downing the rest of it in one gulp.

I can only watch in delight as they grow closer, their shameless intentions clear.

Four

Ing.

The power shuts off the moment midnight comes calling. Rides stop and people scream at the sudden change.
We're smothered in darkness for a few moments.

DONG

Red lights illuminate our feet as fog fills the floor. The scent of it is sweet, delectable.

. . .

DING

When the lights flick back to life, everything has changed. Projectors showcase horror movie scenes on the ground. The whining tick of rides purrs back to life, continuing their loops and twirls.

The Ferris Wheel, which was once an array of bright colors has grown dark and menacing. Screams of delight rip through the crowd that is ever growing.

It's Halloween here now, but no less exciting and inviting than it was moments ago.

Now, it looks like I imagined.

DONG

The Mayhem Monsters descend upon us, climbing gates, spilling in from the darkness. A few of them slide on one knee, impossibly fast and sparking from the metal on their knees as they stop in front of guests.

Twenty men pour through the front gate, faces painted a ghastly white, fake blood smeared on their clothes. They wield large knives, slicing them through the air as they find their targets to pleasure.

A group of fairies circle around a man, hiding whatever they're doing to him with their large, green wings.

DING

On the last chime, a stage to our left is illuminated, showcasing Creed standing with the other four men from earlier. They're in their Purge masks, still shirtless and still incredibly hot.

Creed is in the middle, holding a microphone.

We step closer, peering up.

"Hello Monsters, tonight you're in for a treat." His voice blares through the air. "Please partake in all of your wildest fantasies, let all of your inhibitions run wild." His face sweeps the crowd, the neon mask landing pointedly on me. "Fuck on the rides, fuck in the street. Nothing is wrong here. No rules, no laws. Just you and your lack of inhibition. Enjoy yourselves and be safe. It's time for fucking mayhem!" He growls.

The stage ignites, sparklers flying from the base. They crackle overhead.

The moment Creed finishes his speech they all jump

from the stage and all Hell breaks loose in the best way possible. Music slices through the air, electrifying the already grand space. A menacing laugh sounds in multiple directions, I crane my neck around, looking at the sight before me.

People are hanging from the rafters of the enormous Ferris Wheel. A Mayhem Monster adorning a creepy clown mask walks up to a woman and drops his pants. He's rock hard, and she immediately drops to her knees, taking him without a care in the world.

Creed walks towards me, his head tilts, his tan skin glistening with sweat. This is it.

Instead of giving me the attention I so desperately crave he walks past me. "Go have fun Kels, I'll see you later." He teases, promising again.

"WHERE SHOULD WE GO FIRST?" Mandy asks.

I want to ride something. Well, I want to ride a few things, but the swings look like a good place to start. "Swings?" I suggest, pointing down the walkway.

Mandy grabs my hand as we sweep through the crowd. People are everywhere, and our promise is to not separate tonight. Smoke still lingers on the floor, creating a spooky environment.

As we get closer to the ride, we notice something. Everyone on the swings are completely naked. "Should we do it?" I ask.

Mandy rips off her dress, tossing it onto the railing. "Is that even a fucking question?" She grins. Next, she removes her bra. A lacy scarlet push-up that accentuates her already perky breasts. She slips out of her matching panties but keeps on the heels. "You're stunning." I tell her.

She poses, placing her delicate hands under her chin. "Why thank you, darling." Her hands travel to my shoulders. "Now it's your turn."

Mandy knows me so well. No matter how excited I am to be here and no matter how much I'm willing to do tonight, getting undressed in front of a bunch of strangers makes me a little shy. I need to warm up is all.

She scoops off my top and pulls down my skirt, placing them with hers on the rail. As she unfastens the back of my bra, her lips lay a feather-light touch on my neck. My favorite spot.

This isn't a new feeling; we are two single girls living together after all. I run my fingertip along the swell of her breast, circling until I land on her nipple. The rules are that you cannot fuck or mess with other guests unless they're with your party.

Her nipples harden against my fingertips as I gently squeeze them. She groans, dropping to her knees to pull off my underwear. Before standing back up, she plants a warm kiss on my freshly waxed cunt.

"Come on ladies!" The ride operator holds his cock, stroking it as he watches us. "We're never going to get you up in the air if I stare at you any longer."

"He is fucking hot!" Mandy gasps as we rush to our swings. There are single riders and some that have two seats. We opt to sit together. "Did you see him?"

I let out a laugh. "You mean the guy that was stroking his dick, 6 feet tall with tattoos?"

"Smart ass." She jokes. "This place is overflowing with the guys we read about in books. It is fucking insane."

Our feet dangle as we rise high into the sky. The warm breeze brushes over my skin and just as we begin to spin Mandy's fingertips trail up my bare leg to gently rub my clit.

I elicit a moan of pleasure as I return the favor for her. We're so high in the air. Naked. Spinning in circles. With a view that is just as stunning as the feel of her hands on me.

I peek down, watching people fucking everywhere. Benches, grass, rides. Mandy's finger slips inside of me and my whole body shivers. "Mandy!" I moan.

She leans over to me, the cold steel of the chains against her hard nipples. "I just want to see you have the best night of your life."

"I think I already am." I throw my head back in frustration when she stops. "Why are you teasing me?" I whine.

"I can't keep you all to myself." She grins, pulling me in for a kiss. She tastes like fruit. Cherries and oranges and all things sexual.

I'm a shaking, wet mess as we continue to twirl around and around. We giggle and sightsee. The waters shimmer from the pale moonlight, showcasing the gentle waves.

I have a feeling that's the only gentle thing I'm going to experience tonight.

We gaze at the grounds, trying to take a peek at what's in store. We're still towards the front, so mostly just people and vendors. Some more rides, the games at the far end are too far to tell what they are.

The Ferris Wheel is enormous and smack dab in the middle of the fairgrounds. It's going to give us a much better vantage point to see what the swings don't show.

The rest of the ride is spent in laughter, enjoying ourselves already.

Five

This is our playground for the evening, a world apart from our hectic schedules and overbearing bosses. It doesn't take long to slip our clothes back on and I'm surprised by how comfortable I felt without them.

The neon lights and pulsating music create an intoxicating backdrop as we venture deeper into the fairgrounds.

Past the swings, we notice a wide tent next door. Swaths of bright pink and neon purple surround it. Someone who looks like a bouncer stands outside the cloth door. "What is this?" I ask curiously.

The man -who is wearing sunglasses at night- peers down to look at me. "Mayhem strip club, would you like to go in?"

"Absolutely!" Mandy and I sing in unison.

"Remember," he grins, drawing open the curtain. "touch the strippers."

I squeal, the exact opposite of what the rules are outside of this insane, dreamland.

Enticing dance music flows through the speakers, sending chill bumps down my skin. Fabric walls surround us, a tapestry of patterns. The center stage is ignited with lights, casting an alluring glow that shimmers against the dancers. Theatre lights hang above, displaying gorgeous women dancing on matte black poles.

We sit at the front, watching as they expertly slide up and down. My eyes are drawn to a woman with honey-brown hair. She is captivating. Her skin glistens with a sheen of sweat as she moves her hips sensually against the cool metal pole, using the rhythm of the thumping music to entice the crowd.

Her long leg juts out and she turns, wrapping it around the pole, defying gravity as she moves up and begins to spin around it. Her gaze sweeps the crowd as she spins, sultry eyes and ruby red lips that blow kisses to us.

We peer to our right as the dancers finish their set, taking a bow and exiting the stage. There's a section just for lap dances, and it looks like a marvelous time.

"I want a lap dance stat!" Mandy strides over to an empty chair and sits. Not a moment later a woman is on her lap, grinding and grinning at her.

I take a seat beside Mandy in one of the velvety red chairs, waiting for my turn. Luckily enough, the gorgeous woman with honey-brown hair straddles me.

Her fingertips trail my collarbone as she grinds her hips, swaying them in a maddening motion. I smile, remembering that I don't have to keep my hands to myself. I run my fingertips up along the soft skin of her back until I reach her hair, trapping it in my grip and pulling her toward me.

She smiles, meeting my lips with hers. Our hands are all over each other as her tongue slides into my mouth. She tastes sweet, forbidden. The pressure of her body against mine makes me feel like there's nothing else around us.

I'm completely lost in her touch.

Just as quickly as she came, she's gone again. Leaving me breathless.

From the corner of my eye, I see a man walking towards me. His impressive body makes me bite my lip. Long hair, smothered in tattoos, hot as hell. "Want a ride?" He asks, a thick accent to his deep tone.

I nod, gazing up at him. He throws me over his shoulder and Mandy squeals in delight as he steals me away. "Permission to touch you?"

"Granted!" I shout as he walks up the steps to the stage, pulsating lights disorient me as he flips me over and sets me down on a wooden chair.

What ensues next is nothing short of perfection.

Cherry Pie blares through the speakers as he twirls his hair around, covering me in it. It smells divine, like suntan lotion and coconuts. The man smells like summer. I can't help but run my hands through it when he straddles me.

"Who's ready for a show!" He yells out, stretching his muscular arms out. Behind him I see everyone lining up in front of the stage, Mandy is there with the sexy stripper hanging on her.

His hips grind hard against me, eliciting a moan from my parted lips. He's wearing a little black speedo with a bow tie around his neck.

If your groom was okay with you fucking everyone in sight before the wedding, this would be the best bachelorette destination.

His massive cock is threatening to break free from the thin fabric he's wearing. I run my fingertips along his impressive arms. He's a boulder of masculine energy and I'm here for it.

I smack his ass when he turns around, twerking on me, making me laugh. A few of the female strippers flank me, their hands running through my hair, down my arms, cupping my breasts. I've never been touched by so many people at once, it's an overwhelming sensation that excites me.

The monster of a man stands and rips off his underwear, his dick bouncing out. A murmur of gasps and 'Oh's' escape from the crowd. "Do we think she can do it? Take all of it?" he asks them.

"Yes!" Mandy cheers.

His strong hands grip the chair, and he turns me sideways so the crowd can have a better view. "I can do it, I have no gag reflex." I assure him with a cocky tone. Giving head is one of my most practiced conquests. I always love the look on a man's face when I take all of him in.

This makes him smile. He shoves himself deep down my throat, moaning as he does so. His fingertips brush my neck where his cock sits. "Look at her!" I hear his muffled accent through the hollers and cheers, "Such a good girl." He coos, pulling himself out of me and planting a gentle kiss on my lips.

I stand and bow to the crowd, laughing as Mandy jumps up and down.

My favorite dancer hands him a bottle of chocolate syrup. "Now for your prize!" He grins.

Mandy is brought up on stage with me, and we watch in awe as the man pours the sauce all over his dick.

We get on either side, lapping up the sweet syrup and loving every moment of the entire club cheering us on.

Six

Now, we're heading to the Ferris Wheel.

It's a massive structure, drenched in menacing darkness that would only make sense for Mayhem Carnival. Crackling lights move up and down the wheel's steel framework, igniting the monsters in a here-and-gone glow as they climb around them but their makeup glows in the dark, leaving a trace of their face even after the light leaves.

The gondolas don't bask in the same eerie darkness. They're brightly lit by various neon colors that pulsate and strobe. I see a Mayhem Monster climbing into one as it sways high in the air, I can only imagine what they're getting up to.

Mandy nods her head to a sign. "Single riders only."

"Interesting." I gulp.

She shrugs. "Sucks, I was hoping to tease you again."

I roll my eyes at her. "You've done enough of that tonight."

The line moves at a steady pace and with every inch, anticipation grows. I look at Mandy, her beautiful face illuminated by the carnival lights, eyes wide in delight as the ride operator – painted in zombie make-up – shows us which buckets to climb into.

Mine is bright pink, Mandy is right behind me in a purple one. The groan of the wheel turning makes me hold on tight.

As I ascend, my heart leaps into my chest. *Calm down, Kels.* I take in a few deep breaths before carefully leaning over to the side.

The view is nothing short of breathtaking.

The carnival grounds grow smaller as I go higher, showcasing the twinkling lights and vibrant colors that we've been dancing through for the past hour. Like a dollhouse that I could reach my hand down and grab whatever I wanted. The sweet fog lingers between groups of people.

To my left is where we came in, the harbor beyond it. It allows for a gentle breeze to cascade against my skin like a warm blanket. Behind me is the games. I see spinning wheels, booths, food, and some more rides. I'm so excited for every inch that Mayhem cares to offer us.

To my right, is the Woodline.

With each rotation, I experience a new sight.

Far off in the distance, I spot the corner of the carnival tent, hidden behind brush and a swarm of tree limbs in the woods. It's the last adventure we're going on before we leave.

Just as I inch closer to the edge, to see more of this elusive red and white tent, inked fingers curl around the gondola's basket.

I've been so busy looking out, that I forgot the Monsters were crawling all over the impressive height of the wheel. The man jumps in with ease, his gorgeous face covered in zombie makeup. Black liner surrounds his big green eyes, a shadow of midnight surrounding them.

"You're the least scary zombie I've ever seen," I tell him.

He lets a little smirk slip through his intentionally scary demeanor. "I'm so fucking hungry." He growls.

I tilt my head, "Are you?" He nods his head to my lap. "Do whatever you want to me."

He drops in front of me, his knees pressed against the rubber floor of the basket.

His movements are rigid. Quick, and then slow. He's playing his part well. Zombie pulls his lip between his white teeth as he reaches his hands up to tug my skirt to my waist. I jerk up against the cool plastic seat on my ass and just as I do, he rips my panties off, tossing them in his pocket.

His lips are warm against my leg as he plants kisses all the way up to my inner thigh.

I throw my head back in pleasure as the warm sensation of his tongue flicking over my clit throws my body into a euphoric shock.

Before I know it, both of my legs are over his shoulders.

As he growls against me, my body begins to vibrate, completely out of control. I run my finger through his thick hair, gripping and bucking against him as I orgasm. A night of teasing has made it easy for him.

He takes one last lick before leaping from the basket. I quickly lean over, gasping for breath. "You stole my panties!" I shout playfully.

Like an acrobat, he jumps from rafter to rafter in a terrifying leap before reaching more of his zombies in the middle.

He gives me one last glance, licking his lips with a grin.

I smile, looking down at Mandy. Her long legs are spread wide, heels resting on opposite sides of the gondola. A man is between them, lapping her up. I enjoy seeing her in so much pleasure, the way her head throws back as she moans, gripping the zombie's hair to bury him further into her cunt.

Seven

Mandy meets me on the ground, her hair a disheveled mess.

"That was fucking intense." I finally say, breaking our silence.

She nods quickly, "Professional pussy lickers." She laughs, fixing her hair. "I mean really, where do they find their monsters?"

I would love to know that because if that zombie came over weekly, I would be a lot less stressed out day to day.

I was worried things would move too quickly, but we're just now nearing the end of the first street. Right next to the strip club sits an array of colorful carnival games. A long stretch of booths and tents, awaiting us to play.

"Come here!" Someone shouts.

"Guaranteed prize!" Another sings at a booth showcasing one of the monsters getting a butt plug shoved into her by a blindfolded woman. I look at the sign at the table. 'Pin the plug in the lady.' A play of pin the tail on the donkey.

A laugh escapes me, "That is too funny."

"Looks fun too!" Mandy agrees, giggling. "But we're going here."

Kissing Booth

MANDY PUSHES me through a crowd of people to a set of steps. An adorable kissing booth is adorned with a colorful banner, draped in blue suede curtains.

A Mayhem Monster, dawning an eerie imitation of a phantom mask that covers his face is wearing a black tuxedo, holding out a sprawling red rose. The butterflies dance in my stomach excitedly. As nasty as I like to be, I enjoy romance. The cheesy, sweet kind that makes you melt.

As I reach for the rose the phantom gently sweeps me into his embrace, bending me back in a sweeping curl as he plants his warm, plump lips on mine.

Chills rise on my skin as his tongue dances with mine.

Bright fireworks spark at the corners of the small stage. He lifts me back up, giving me an elaborate bow.

This booth is probably the sweetest thing at the carnival.

I squeal when I get to Mandy, "That was adorable! Your turn!"

She shakes her head, "Very cute, but not my thing. I want to do this!"

Ring Toss

The carnival worker is animated, standing on the counter to gather attention. "Come one, come all! One ring on a cock wins a prize!"

A black and white wall about three feet high separates us from what's in the booth. "Here you go, ladies!" The man smiles, handing us each three glowing plastic rings. I set my red rose on the counter, ready to take aim.

Instead of bottles lined on shelves, there are men sitting on tables, their backs against a wall and their dicks erect. A woman stands by, sucking and jacking them when they go soft, which is rare assuming every man here has taken a truckload of Viagra.

Mandy's competitive nature is igniting, "Bet you I'll make two." She challenges.

I toss the disc. It flies in the air, landing on one of the men's stomachs. "Damn it!" I shout.

Mandy giggles, tossing hers with ease and cheering as it slides down the shaft of the same guy. "One down." She sings.

My next toss is a miss, and Mandy's of course isn't. I root for her although right now, she's the competition. "Last one." I let out a breath and we toss our rings simultaneously. They click together, and gravity does the work, tumbling them to the ground. "Ah!" I yawn, struggling to handle all of this excitement.

"What prizes would you like? You pick two" The man asks, his hand sweeps in a flourish to the walls adorned with various toys.

"Hmm," Mandy purrs, looking down at my rose. "I'll take the rose and the pink handcuffs."

She hands the rose to me. It's a small, handheld vibrator, silicone soft. "For you." She tells me.

"Aww no, I lost!" I grin.

"I have to win you something, we're on a date right now." She winks.

The man offers us a bag, "Anything you win during your games place in here and at the end of your games you'll see a black booth, go there to drop it off."

Mayhem thinks of everything. "Thank you!" We tell him, stepping away to see what else there is to play.

"Oh! Look at that!" I point.

Seven Minutes in Heaven
Mandy POV

THE SIGN READS, 'Can you last seven minutes?'

There are whips and chains lining the banister.

This is my shit.

"Want to partake? Or watch?" I ask Kels, nodding to a chair that sits on the side. A glass partition in front of it. She's getting tired, though she won't admit it. I'll get her a coffee, maybe some food and she'll perk right up.

She sends me a sly smile, "I want to watch, I need to get off of my feet for a minute." *Told you.*

I hand her our bag of goodies and step to the door where a woman sits on a bar stool.

"Read the sign." She says flatly, her nail jutting to a plaque.

RULES

. . .

1. Entering grants full permission for anything to happen.
2. Whips, chains, dildos, and other tools are in use.
3. The safe word is "CARNIVAL!"

"AGREED." I sing as she pushes the door open. I step inside, jumping as it slams closed, leaving me in the pitch black.

This isn't the nice, sweet booth Kels experienced with the phantom. This is what Mayhem is all about.

I'm swept up by someone, my dress is taken off of me in an instant as he bends me over, rubbing lube on my cunt.

A sharp sting slaps my ass, the familiar feeling of a paddle. I yelp in delight, begging for more.

The darkness makes this all the more exciting, and as I'm grabbed again, being thrown around like a doll, I moan.

I'm being fucked from behind, face against a cold wall when the lights blare to life. It takes me a moment to gather my senses, and then I see Kels on the other side, her lips parted, watching.

A smile sweeps over my face as she touches herself.

My body jerks back, and then up. I'm lifted into the air,

wrapping my legs around the waist of a man made of muscle. His cock slides into me at a rapid pace.

There are four men off to the side, all wearing clown masks, stroking themselves. "Want to say the safe word?" One sneers, trying to scare me.

I grip the man's shoulders and bounce myself on his dick, showing them all just how ready I am. "Not at all." I purr.

They all come after me, pulling me from the man and tossing my shaking body onto a cold, steel table. I moan in pleasure as one stuffs his cock into my pussy, while another fills my mouth. Laying down and looking up at five terrifying-looking clowns is now my newest, greatest fantasy. I can't believe this is happening.

A neon clock showcases the time. I have to last for four more minutes. "Harder!" I shout out when my mouth is free for a moment. My feet are being swatted at with a bamboo stick, my hands both jacking off two of the clowns.

Something penetrates deep into my ass, and I cry out. Not daring to say the words they're trying to get me to say.

I could do this all fucking night.

I peek over at Kels, who is watching us with utter fascination.

I give her a smile before my throat is grabbed.

Air leaves my lungs, making my body twitch in delight.

My body goes through a few stages of euphoria as I'm pounded by complete and total strangers.

DING! The clock chimes, and everyone pulls out of me. They all take off their masks, showcasing model-like faces. Strong jaw lines and sincere gazes. "You're the only one who's made it tonight so far!" One says proudly.

Another grabs a wet cloth and wipes me down. "Here," A man with green eyes and dark stubble hands me a brush. Another, a glass of water.

"You did amazing." He says.

I grin at them. "Thank you."

I jump from the table, not daring to let them see how wobbly they've made me. I am way too competitive for that. "This booth has the biggest prizes," Green Eyes grins, bringing me to a wall of heavy-duty vibrators. He nods his head to the window, "Your friend gets one too."

I pick out two fancy-looking ones, and he hands me the boxes before escorting me to Kels. I pass by the woman on the bar stool and she gives me an appreciative nod.

"Got you another present!" I smile when I round the corner.

Kels looks me over, "Are you okay? That was fucking intense."

I take the bag from her, sliding both boxes in. "That was the greatest moment of my life." I tell her. "and I'm the only one who has lasted all seven minutes!"

Kels points to the next booth raising her brows, "There's a glory hole game."

Glory Hole
Kels

"Do you want a cock in your ass, pussy, or mouth?" The woman asks in the sweetest voice. We may as well play everything, right? I mean, Mandy just put in some work, so I need to win her something too.

Mandy tilts her head, weighing her options.

On the other side of the wall are seven holes. Mandy, me and one other woman are readying ourselves. Three of the seven men will be getting a prize.

I place my mouth near the hole, readying myself.

Mandy bends her long body over, her legs so tall she nearly can't place herself properly and the other woman lies on a bed with her legs against the wall.

"There are three holes filled on this side." The woman smirks in our direction. "When I finish my countdown, I want those rock-hard fucking cocks jammed in, do you understand? In three!" The woman shouts, and I can imagine the throbbing cocks on the other side, waiting for their chances. "Two!" A man moans on the other side in pleasure. From what I've seen there are men and women walking around and keeping people's dicks hard.

"One!"

Mandy yelps out a moan of pleasure just as I take someone into my mouth. It's warm and large.... very large. I laugh as four other cocks are sprung through the holes with nowhere to go. It's empowering hearing the guys on the other end root and cheer for being inside of us.

"Prizes awarded for winners and participants!" The woman sings.

I laugh at the selection, the most normal thing tonight. "I'll take the pink bear." I decide.

"Blue one!" Mandy points, looking at me. We drop our bags at the booth and they scan our QR codes.

Mandy wraps her arm in mine. "How about a coffee and then a ride?"

"Yes! We need a break from everything." I lie, wanting more, wanting everything there is. Why couldn't this be a three-day event?

Eight

Mandy and I approach the Gravitron. The massive chamber spins, its lights pulsating and illuminating our skin in a blue hue as we wait in line. I sip the coffee Mandy got for me, relishing in the warm caffeinated beverage and praying that I don't hurl it back up after this ride.

The spaceship-like doors finally open and the carnival-goers stumble out, some dizzy and others euphoric. I wonder what kind of mayhem happens here.

Inside is a different world, metal flanks the floor, ceiling, and walls. Like the rest of the night, people are either half-dressed, fully naked, or like me, still clothed. Well, aside from the underwear the worker on the Ferris Wheel kept.

The control panel in the middle holds the Mayhem Monsters.

Ten of them.

Five women and Five men.

The girls are maskless, showcasing their striking beauty. We all go to our standing seats.

The metal doors creak closed behind us, smothering the chamber in darkness as we begin a slow spin.

Music begins to bump, red lights flicker from the roof. The monsters are hanging on the sides of the control panel, safe from the G-forces that are now beginning to pin the riders in place.

Mandy and I laugh as gravity pushes us back, holding our bodies on the cushioned wall.

Impossibly, the monsters start walking sideways, using the spinning motion to keep them upright. I couldn't work in here, it's fun to ride in but doing this all night? No way.

A Ghost Face monster is heading straight for me, menacingly tilting his head. He jumps down, the pull of gravity colliding our bodies together.

"Cock warm for me?" He asks.

I size him up. Six feet tall with broad shoulders, but I can't see much else. It's too dark in here.

"Absolutely." I grin.

The operator goes over the loudspeaker. "We don't want any cum flying around at mock speed, so make sure to finish in your condom, in their mouths, or on the towels provided."

"Where do you want it?" Ghost Face asks. His body rubbing up against mine, cock hardened and ready for me.

I think for a moment, wondering about the logistics. "Condom." I decide.

"Your wish is my command." He mutters over the loud music.

He slides it over himself and shoves my skirt up to my stomach. A bottle of lube in his hand, Ghost Face smothers it all over the condom. With a flick of his wrist, the operator turns the speed up.

He lines the tip of his cock with my soaking-wet opening. Flashing lights make the space feel like a nightclub and the gravitational force helps him to slide his massive cock as far as humanly possible inside of me in a matter of seconds. I yelp out a moan.

When he said cock warm, I assumed that's all that would be physically possible, but as I look around I see Mandy getting fucked.

To my other side is a woman, a girl between her legs licking and sucking on her clit. Beside her, a man is being fucked from behind. The world blurs into a twinkling whirlwind of neon lighting as the ride reaches its peak.

I toss my head back from the sight of so much ecstasy as Ghost Face barrels in and out of me. My hands slide around his strong arms. Feeling the bulge of his veins through his soft black t-shirt as he pulls himself in and out as we spin faster and faster.

I thought this ride would make me nauseous, but fuck this is intense and incredible.

"Choke me." I tell him, wanting some of what Mandy experienced earlier.

Without hesitation, he slides his inked hand up, carefully so as to not collapse my throat but enough to make me see stars, which is what I wanted.

We both climax together as the ride begins to slow, allowing him to have better movement.

His hips sway in a maddening motion as I run my hands along his broad shoulders.

That was powerful, fucking powerful.

Nine

The enticing aroma of street food fills the air, making my stomach growl. "We need to replenish."

Mandy nods, "Who knew a night of euphoria could be so exhausting?"

We walk down the busy walkway; the tantalizing scent of different foods makes my hunger grow to new heights. Vendors are lined up on both sides. Food and refreshments on the entire back strip.

We walk up to a booth that's in the shape of a bottle of mustard, "Can I have the penis-shaped corn dog, please?" I laugh.

"Same!" Mandy declares, "Oh! Also, the chocolate-covered cock."

I look at her, "Will a guy come out…"

"No," She laughs, gesturing to the woman who is dipping a banana in a pot of melted, sweet chocolate.

"You know, with all the dick-shaped stuff this is like a bachelorette party." I say.

The woman hands us our items and I can't stop laughing at my corn dog. It's huge, twelve inches, and covered in a thick batter. The balls near the bottom are two hush puppies stuck to the sides with toothpicks.

Mandy takes a bite of hers. "Can you imagine if someone came here for a bachelorette for real?"

I walk over to the drink station and grab a big bottle of water. Not paying for anything is pretty nice. "There wouldn't be a wedding if the groom found out. I was thinking about that earlier, at the strip club tent. Like, if their husband was cool enough to let them have one last getaway before being tied down to one guy their whole lives that would be great." We giggle as we scarf down our food like ravaged beasts.

"Oh my god," I mumble with a mouthful.

Mandy catches what I'm staring at, holding out the banana for me to take a bite.

There are five tables, a person lying on each of them with various foods on their bodies. A woman is grabbing a piece of sushi off a woman's breast with her mouth.

We walk over towards the tables after finishing our food and I go straight for an onion ring that's stacked covering a man's dick. I dip down and grab it with my teeth. Mandy goes to the table next to me, with a man who feeds you raw oysters on a shell. He's sitting up, his legs covered with lemons and crackers. She slurps the oyster up and he squirts a squeeze of lemon on her tongue before kissing her.

This was the break we needed, an hour of food and hydration to prepare ourselves for the rest of our unforgettable evening.

Ten

We pull out our trusty map, "Here's where we're going next." I point down the last road. This one houses the last two places we're visiting tonight. The Haunted House, then the Circus Tent.

The long stretch of street is nearly empty, a few stragglers make their way from the exit of the Haunted House, but it seems like most of the guests are back at the main attractions.

I pull her hand to a gate at the woodline. "We're going in the woods?" Mandy tugs on my hand, letting out a quick breath.

"Don't be scared." I tell her. She's one of the bravest people I know, but when it comes to the woods, she is a chicken. We went tent camping once, and she made me sleep in the car with her in case we needed to escape. "Just think about all of the hot guys who want to make us scream."

"Oh," She purrs, "I like the sound of that."

I lead her in, "Just remember, after this is the Carnival Tent and then we're done, so let's enjoy the most of these last two adventures."

Mandy is trying to not look terrified as we walk down the dimly lit trail, but she's failing. "What if there's like a serial killer that snuck in?"

I laugh, pointing her attention to the Mayhem Monsters lurking in the woods, a flicker of their signature wristbands lets us know it's them. Red lights that are flush with the forest floor show us a glimpse of their shadows. "Then one of those guys will save us. I promise you, we're safe. Enjoy this, Mandy. Seriously."

The exciting sounds and bright lights of the fairgrounds are long gone from here. It's replaced by an inky darkness, eerie silence, and thick fog that lingers at our feet.

The canopy of trees above allows the moon to barely penetrate through. I know it's regulated, and that we're in no actual danger, but the ambiance for fear is on point and my heart rate is growing faster with every step we take.

An owl hoots in the distance, but it doesn't sound like an animal. Another distant hoot lets us know that it's not. My eyes pan the woodline again, watching as the men make their way, not to us, but following our path.

Damp earth invades my nostrils as we navigate the trail. Mandy bumps into me and we both let out a chuckle of nervous laughter. A rustle in a nearby bush captures our attention and we both pick up the pace.

Mandy is surveying the men as I try to stay on the path. She pulls her lip between her teeth, watching them. "I figured it out." She says, gesturing to the wooded area. "The theme for the Haunted House is psychopaths but sexy."

She's referring to the men wielding knives, staring at us from the cover of dark trees. The red lights have grown more sparse, illuminating their chilling glares when they step over them. "Yeah, the zombie earlier was so fucking hot he could have eaten my brains and I wouldn't have cared."

She laughs, "From the sounds of it I wouldn't doubt he ate you."

I playfully swat her arm as we walk down the trail looking for the Haunted House. We round a bend, catching sight of a man standing ten feet away. He's in a white t-shirt and camo pants, drenched in blood. A hunter's hat lies on his head, knife in hand. We take a small step forward, and he mirrors us.

I look back, hearing footsteps crunching on the fallen

leaves, but no one is there. Mandy stiffens, quickening her pace as we rush past the man who stays put, not following anymore.

Suddenly, the red lights shut off in the woodline. It was already hard to see and now it's impossible. "Where is this fucking house?" I ask her.

"Run." A voice whispers between us.

"We're in it!" I figure it out, following the orders of whoever was just breathing down our necks.

"Hey Monsters, we've got two runners!" Someone yells from our left, his knife glinting in the sliver of moonlight.

The trees light up, dazzling sparkles amid chaos that gives us a fighting chance to see where we're going, to play this game to our advantage. "You're being hunted." An eerie voice sings as we hide behind a tree. I look to Mandy, checking on her. "You okay?"

"Fuck yes." She grins.

We rush to another tree, ducking behind its low-hanging branches, trying to catch sight of who is hunting us.

Five men are walking slowly, looking around. "So, this is epic." I whisper.

Mandy cups her face, "I wonder what they're going to do with us!" She squeals, alerting our location.

A split second later she's pulled away from me.

Two of the men have her pinned to a nearby tree, a grin spreading from ear to ear on her face as one places the knife to her throat. Another one grabs my arm. "Uh uh." A voice sounds and the man releases me.

A creak sounds above and I'm unable to run before a figure jumps down from the branch, a loud thud sounds as his black boots land in front of my feet. I peer up, smiling when I see a familiar blue mask.

"I told you I'd find you," Creed growls, he points his attention at the other monsters. "This one's mine boys."

"More for me!" Mandy sings, letting me know it's okay to step away. Creed grabs my hand and leads me to a clearing far enough away from everyone else for some privacy. He lies me on a blanket of lush grass.

"You're fucking stunning." He breathes, looking me over.

I run my fingertip along the stitched mouth of his glowing mask, "Let me see you." I beg.

His inked fingers tuck underneath the plastic and when he pulls it off, tossing it beside us, my breath ceases to exist.

"*You're* fucking stunning." I say back to him. Admiring the crystal blue of his eyes, thankful for the shimmering white lights in the trees that allow me to experience this moment.

His chiseled jawline frames a strong face, with high cheekbones and olive skin. Black hair that's in a beautiful mess lies haphazardly just above his thick brows.

But those eyes. Those blue eyes that are flanked by jealousy-inducing lashes steal every morsel of my attention.

He smiles, and it's infectious. "Have you had a good night?"

"It's better now that you're here," I tell him.

The softness of his full lips on mine is a much-needed change from the rough night I've had. It's been perfect, don't get me wrong but as I said, I do enjoy romance. Lying with him under the moonlight with only the sounds of rustling trees is the best way I could think to end the night before we go to the Carnival Tent.

I bask in his embrace, the way our tongues dance and twirl together in harmony.

His fingers curl underneath my top and he lifts it, burying his face into my breasts. Gently sucking my nipples and moving to plant kisses along my neck.

I move my hands to the bulge in his pants, beginning to stroke him. Aside from the Gravitron, this entire night has been foreplay and I'm ready for the real thing.

"I'm so happy you found me." I moan into his mouth.

His warm hand dips between my legs, fingers teasing me. "I've been waiting."

I moan as he gently circles my clit with his fingertip, kissing my neck while he drives me wild. A moment later his lips are traveling to plant kisses down my chest, his body slips between my legs. He replaces his finger with his tongue, twirling it around.

My hands run through his hair, relishing in the feel of his warm mouth against me. I tug up, begging for him.

He refuses to move, sending my body into a flurry of bliss. I lift my hips, allowing his hands to travel to my ass. He squeezes and grabs, burying his face deeper.

Finally, when I'm about to come undone, he travels back up to me. I taste myself on his lips.

I place my hands on his strong shoulders, turning him so he's lying on his back. I straddle his thighs and stroke him, watching the way he's hungrily eying my body.

There's a condom in his left hand. I steal it, ripping it open with my teeth.

He writhes below me, unzipping and pulling his pants off quickly. His cock bounces out, freeing from the constraints of his boxers as he pulls them down too.

A seductive grin takes over me as I push the condom down his shaft before lifting up to slide him inside of me.

He lets out a low growl, gripping my hips to help. "This is the best ride of the night." I tell him with a moan, throwing my head back from the sensation of being filled as I bounce up and down.

His hands cup my breasts, my hips, everywhere. He adores every inch of my body, sitting up to feel more of me.

After a few moments, he flips me over, hands squeezing hard on my breasts as he pounds inside of me. We've been like this for a long while. Entangled, moaning, panting messes.

His hips twirl, allowing himself to enter deeper. He's calm and collected now. With one final shove, he pulls out, tossing the condom aside and spilling his load into my mouth. I swallow him up, drinking him in as the night comes to a near close.

One more place to go, but the only thing I want to do is stay here, with him.

Creed's fingertips trail my jawline as I catch my breath on the cool, dewy grass, smiling at him.

Suddenly, the ground begins to glow. Amber bulbs ignite a pathway, enticing us to follow.

Creed scoops me up from the ground, "Ready for the finale?"

Eleven

Hand in hand, we walk down the lit pathway. I could try to play it cool, but my wide grin gives away how giddy I feel.

I can't get over how handsome Creed is or how special he's made me feel tonight. "Do you tell all the girls you'll find them?" I ask, frowning. "And then you fuck them in the woods and take them to the carnival?"

He laughs and it echoes off the trees. I turn back to catch sight of Mandy who is being escorted by two of the men. She's holding one of their fake knives. "I've only been with you tonight." He tells me, running his thumb against my hand.

My frown turns around. "Really?"

"Mhmm." He purrs. "A few times."

I stop in my tracks, tilting my head in inquiry. "Huh?"

"Gravitron." He grins. "It was so fun fucking you on that ride." He throws his head back, recalling the memory with a tilt of his lip. I'm speechless as he bends, bowing. "Also, Phantom."

The sweet, gentle man with the mask who gave me the rose. Ghost Face that fucked me hard on the ride. "How could I not have known?"

He shrugs, "Costumes, we have the best artist here and I made sure I was where you would be."

"Have you been following me, Creed?"

He bats his lashes, "If I say yes, will you hold it against me?"

I blush. "I'll hold myself against you anytime."

"Oh, the glory hole too." He grins.

I swat his arm. "You didn't let anyone else around me." I tease, not caring in the slightest bit. "I can't believe you scaled the Ferris Wheel."

"Uh, about that." He pauses, "I wasn't climbing that fucking thing."

The quiet forest fills with our laughter. I knew he wasn't the zombie, I would have recognized him the moment he pulled off his mask if he was. Not that the zombie wasn't handsome, it's just that Creed is in another world. Delectable.

His hand lifts, bringing mine with it. "Welcome to Mayhem Carnival."

A colossal red and white tent comes into view as we round a corner. We're not at the front, this is a different entrance. I know because I hear chatter way on the other end where a line must be, and two stadium lights that shoot into the sky accompany the noise. "How did they even get this thing here?"

He waves his hands in front of his face, opening a curtain. "Magic."

He's not wrong, it's tucked into the woods, flanked by sprawling trees. I step in, enveloped by a crowd of people. Mandy is on our heels. "I'm taking you into the cast entrance." He says.

"Oh, why thank you, Sir." I do a small curtsy, trying not to fall as a woman rushes by half-dressed and tugging on another outfit. "It's busy here!"

"Dressing room." One of the guys with Mandy calls out.

Creed leads me to the middle, where racks of clothes are sprawled out. Various costumes are being strewn about, passed between carnival workers.

A woman steps onto a box near us, "Call time!"

Everyone moves like worker bees, bustling around us at a speed that I can't keep up with. Mandy grips my hand during the commotion at the exact moment that I'm pulled away from Creed by a group of noisy mimes.

"We need to get out of here," I tell her, noticing a flurry

of commotion coming from the corner of the room that's making its way to us.

Mandy and I escape the dressing room through a side door, spilling out into the main area of the carnival tent.

We're both in awe as we look up to a sprawling ceiling of red and white fabric. It drapes impossibly high in the middle of the ceiling, flowing outward to hug the walls.

At the center is a long, glossy black stage, surrounded by bleachers. A woman holds a microphone, gathering everyone's attention.

Dazzling lights flicker around, music blares, a symphony of sounds slicing through the air. "We would like to introduce the owner, operator, the fucking legend of Mayhem Carnival... The King!" Creed runs out, dressed in a black suit. His dark hair is slicked back. "Creed Mayhem!"

He turns to me as he addresses the crowd. "Thank you for joining our hourly event! I know some of you have been waiting for me at the other showings, but I was busy stalking a guest." He chuckles, and the crowd follows his laughter. "We have an amazing show for you tonight. Enjoy." He bows, walking backward until he's swallowed up by the curtain.

The air is charged. A murmur of excitement spills through the crowd as the lights dim and the show begins. A spotlight blares to life high in the air, revealing a group of acrobats that fly above our heads from ring to ring. They hang on to each other and my breath catches in my throat as they drop down, I hold it until they are grabbed by their partners.

Some are naked, others dressed in fairy costumes. I watch as some of them fuck from the rafters.

They fly, sending chills across my skin. It looks so real, although I can see the gleam from the thin rope that keeps them safe. Their movements are as flawless as a ballet recital.

The mimes, who were quite chatty earlier come out in silence, putting on a hilarious performance.

This show is spectacular, a meticulously planned symphony of talent.

Magicians spill into the crowd, dazzling us with their tricks.

Finally, a woman in a purple gown that shimmers all on its own steps out, singing a melody that seems to put the crowd in a trance. She's enchanting.

"Look up." The singer says once she finishes, pointing to an illuminated neon rope that sits taut from end to end.

Creed walks out above us, wearing a velvet black cape, his phantom mask is back on. There's nothing attached to him, no safety lines or net below to catch him if he falls.

I sit on the edge of my seat as fear and anticipation swirl around me. The gasps of the guests don't help to tame my worries as he begins his tightrope walk.

His arms are stretched out, keeping his balance as he steadily walks across.

Finally, he reaches the end and I take a few long, deep breaths to calm myself down. Just as suddenly, he drops.

He's hanging onto the line with one hand waving. A wide grin is on his face as he teases the crowd.

He begins to swing himself back and forth, gaining momentum until he can reach one of the acrobat's metal rings. With the precision of a professional, he scurries down each obstacle, landing on his feet on the stage. The crowd erupts in applause.

"For our last few performances, we're going to need a participant. I would like to invite Kelsey to the stage." People murmur, their heads whipping around to see who will be entertaining them.

I stand, walking towards Creed who is now holding his hand out for me.

I step onto the stage, trying to hide a blush that rises to my cheeks. Before I can make it to that handsome man with those deep blue eyes, I'm swept away by a woman in a tight black cat costume.

She brings me behind the curtain to the dressing area and plops me down on a chair. A group of people surround me, getting to work with my hair and make-up.

"You ready for this?" Creed asks, coming up behind me. I see his handsome reflection in the mirror. He's no longer in his phantom outfit. Black jeans and a black T-shirt make for a lip-biting sight.

I let out a laugh as a man sweeps mascara over my lashes, "I don't know what I'm supposed to be ready for exactly." I hear the distant sounds of laughter as a comedian entertains the audience with jokes.

With three people curling my blond streaks, it only takes moments for them to finish. They spritz my hair with spray and hurry me to the clothing rack.

I'm placed into a tight, diamond-encrusted bodysuit with matching, shimmering shoes. I take a quick look in the mirror, admiring how ethereal I look. "You guys are magicians, seriously."

Creed loops my arm through his, walking us over to the large black curtain. A flurry of butterflies dance through my stomach as I'm overloaded with uncertainty in the best way possible. "Have you ever had a knife thrown at your head?" He asks just as the curtains drop.

The stage lights blind me momentarily, but when I focus I see Mandy staring at me in awe. Probably wishing we could bring the glam team home with us to New York from my sudden change of appearance.

To my right, Creed guides me to a large wheel. "Lean here." He instructs. I would jump off a bridge if this man told me to, which is dangerous I know, but he's so damn good-looking.

I lean against the wooden wheel, knowing what's coming next. He straps me in at my ankles and wrists before stepping back. "Welcome to the Spinning Wheel of Death!" He shouts into the microphone. Everyone cheers as I begin to twirl in circles.

"Don't move, Kels." He tells me over the microphone.

"I feel like there should have been more training than this!" I shout back playfully but I've been in those very capable hands, and he is the King of Mayhem after all, he knows what he's doing.

The crowd is silent as they wait for a knife to be plunged through my head. Creed's muscular arm lifts up and out. The whir of sharp, gleaming metal slices through the air, landing inches from my face.

And another by my leg.

With each throw, I grow more confident.

But I don't move a centimeter.

The final knife lands right between my legs, inches from my kitty.

Creed comes to release me, gently running his hand between my legs as he undoes my restraints.

The feeling reminds me of all the pleasure I experienced tonight.

I'm struck that there isn't a stage full of people having sex, but really that's the entire point of the fairgrounds. Now, we get to enjoy this wonderful show.

And I'm lucky enough to be *in* it.

The lights dim once again as a man takes away the spinning wheel, replacing it with a large, metal globe.

"The Metal Cage of Death." Creed growls into the microphone before placing it on the stand.

I laugh as he leads me inside, "A lot of death in these names." I tease.

He places his hands on my shoulders, "I need you to stand as stiff as a board, Kels. Can you do that for me?"

I nod, "I trust you." I tell him.

He plants a kiss on my lips before exiting the chamber. I'm surrounded by the confines of a metal ball. The audience cheers when he barrels out of the shadows on a motorcycle and enters beside me. He's wearing a matte black helmet that matches the bike. A leather jacket snug against him.

The engine roars, making the metal floor at my feet vibrate as someone shuts the door, locking it in place. With a turn of his wrist, he begins circling me, slowly and at an incline, working his way around. The engine revs louder, the hunk of metal and motor coming dangerously close to my body.

He gains momentum, the rumble of the motor makes my heart pound the faster he goes.

My favorite part is that as he flips upside down, winding impossibly inches beside my head with the tire, his hand reaches out to gently cup my face.

He's a master of the machine, and he knows it.

The deafening roar of his bike and the dizzying speed is all I can focus on, like it's just me and him and the rest of the world doesn't exist. As he slows, I'm brought back to the present. Without the whirl of his bike overtaking my vision I can see around us now, everyone standing and cheering us on.

He allows me to exit first when the door opens, following me with his bike.

The wheel is taken away, and now I can see the transformation that took place while we were inside.

On the long, sleek black stage sits a large metal circle in the middle, on either side is a ramp. Creed rolls past the curtain, grabs a baton from an outstretched hand that's peeking through, and rides over to me. "You're going to need this." He says, nodding his head to the ring. "Keep your distance." He warns.

A rush of heat warms my skin as he ignites the end.

With a swift hand, he grabs the microphone from the stand, still straddling his bike. "Now we're onto the final act of the night!" I follow his cue, stepping over to the large ring and keeping a safe distance as I walk up the steps and lift the burning baton to its metal frame. It ignites in a deafening whoosh. "The Burning Ring of Fire!"

He lost a really good pun there, the burning ring of death would have been funnier considering the other names.

The baton sizzles as I place it in a nearby bucket of water before returning to the microphone on stage left.

Creed revs the engine, riding towards the edge of stage right. He accelerates fast, jumping the ramp with ease. As he flies through the air I look up in admiration at his talent. The fire moves with his speed as he jumps through the ring and just when I think he's safe, the fire catches on his jacket, igniting him.

He lands on the other ramp, and drops the bike, running to center stage on fire, his hands flailing around.

The woman in the catsuit runs out in a panic, trying to figure out how to use the extinguisher. I quickly grab it from her and pull the pin. I aim it at the fire that engulfs his body, squeezing the handle and spraying him down until theirs nothing left. I toss the canister aside.

A cloud of white overtakes the stage, my heart racing as I search for him.

"Mayhem fucking Carnival thanks you for coming!" Creed bellows through a speaker, stepping out of the white smoke, wearing a black suit.

I rush into his arms, kissing his cheek. "You could have warned me!"

"Where's the fun in that?" He smirks.

All of the performers spill onto the stage, linking arms. Creed and I are at the center of it all.

The stage feels like home, and with each cheer from the audience I grow fonder of it.

Mandy is jumping up and down, freaking out and chanting my name.

I turn to Creed, basking in his gaze. "I never want this night to end." I say to him as we bow.

As sparklers fly, crackling around us, the crowd goes wild. Creed pulls me in close, a feather touch away from my lips. "Do you want to be the Queen of Mayhem?"

About the Author

I created Scarlett Swan when I wanted to write darker romances but didn't want to interfere with my usual New Adult romance content. If you would like to check out more of my work, follow H.L. Swan.

Find other Scarlett Swan works by scanning the QR code below!

Printed in Great Britain
by Amazon